A Stroke of Magic

BOOK 1

THE DINOSAUR WOMAN

A Stroke Of Magic

THE DINOSAUR WOMAN

Brunella Costagliola
illustrated by Valerio Mazzoli

wee b. books

an imprint of W. Brand Publishing

NASHVILLE, TENNESSEE

wee b. books, an imprint of W. Brand Publishing.

j.brand@wbrandpub.com

www.wbrandpub.com

Cover design by designchik.net

Illustrations by Valerio Mazzoli

Publisher's Note: This is a work of fiction. Names, characters, places, and incidents are a product of the author's imagination. Locales and public names are sometimes used for atmospheric purposes. Any resemblance to actual people, living or dead, or to businesses, companies, events, institutions, or locales is completely coincidental.

A Stroke of Magic: The Dinosaur Woman–1st edition

Available in Hardcover, Paperback, eBook, and Kindle

Hardcover ISBN: 978-1-956906-45-5

Paperback ISBN: 978-1-956906-46-2

eBook ISBN: 978-1-956906-47-9

Library of Congress Number: 2022950773

Contents

To Alexander and Rossella,

my most treasured source of inspiration.

Con tanto amore,

Mamma

CHAPTER 1

Discovery Casa

DISCOVERY CASA IN VERO Beach, Florida, was a retirement home like no other. It had everything that its senior residents—and their visitors—could possibly need to have oh-so-much fun when they spent time together.

The outside building was made of turquoise wood siding, and a sign hung on the bright yellow front door read:

WELCOME TO DISCOVERY CASA
IT TOOK US AGES TO GROW YOUNG

The lobby welcomed guests with a soothing ukulele melody of *plink plink chiky plink*. Near the door, a wide variety of gumball machines, one for every gum, candy, surprise, sticker, toy, or tattoo anyone could wish for. A long corridor took guests from the lobby to the open-air plaza, at the center of what seemed to be a whole other town with its own arcade, dance room, library, pool, bocce court, and café, which had the best yummy pastries, muffins, and cakes for every occasion. The buttery smell of freshly baked croissants, deliciously paired with the comforting aroma of hot cocoa, was enough to make every person take a deep breath in, smile, and go *"Mmm!"*

Framed by tall trees, the plaza had several park benches where guests and residents could sit down, chitchat, and admire the fresh flowers around them before going over to their own casa.

Every casa was so much more than just a room; it looked like a real casa, with the name of the resident it housed painted on the mailbox. It even had a porch with two rocking chairs that overlooked a small front yard.

But what made Discovery Casa so unique was its staff, residents, and visitors. Especially Alex, Ella, and Layla.

CHAPTER 2

ALex, Ella, and Layla

ALEX AND ELLA'S MAMMA worked at Discovery Casa as a nurse, and they loved going there with her after school, even though they spent way too many quarters at the gumball machines, played in the arcade till their eyes hurt, and, alas, lost at bocce against the feisty residents.

On a warm Fall afternoon, Alex and Ella walked into the Discovery Casa lobby behind Mamma, who said: "Now, now, don't get into any trouble you two."

"Mamma, we are seven years old," Ella said. "We're big kids now, you don't have to worry about us."

Mamma smiled and gave them a kiss before starting her afternoon shift.

"Race you to the game room!" Alex said when their mamma was no longer in sight.

He took off before Ella even had a chance to sprint into action. He was a fast runner—so fast that she believed his feet had been genetically modified with sonic

3

boosters or something. And as if that wasn't enough, Alex was a fast talker too. That boy could talk just about anything.

With Alex already too far away, Ella decided to try her luck at the gumball machine.

"Suh-weet!" she exclaimed when she saw her prize: a temporary turtle tattoo! She ran to the bathroom, peeled off the plastic top sheet, slightly wet the paper, and with the knowhow of a seasoned tattoo artist, she firmly placed her newest addition on her skin—next to the butterfly and the shark tattoos. After thirty seconds had gone by, she admired her beautifully decorated arm in the mirror and ran off to the game room to show Alex.

"Look what I—" Ella stopped in her tracks when she entered the room and found a girl talking to Alex.

"Oh, there you are," Alex said, looking at his sister. "Ella, this is Layla. She's six and is from Panama but lives in Vero Beach like us and goes to our same school, only she's in first grade. Isn't it weird we've never met? Anyway, her grandmother lives here, Layla wants us to go meet her and then maybe we can all go play bocce," he said without even taking a breath.

"Hi," Ella said, when Alex finally came back up for air. "What's that?" she asked, pointing to a book in Layla's hands.

"It's my Discovery Diary," she said, showing it to them. "My cousins sent it to me from Panama, so I can draw

and write everything I discover here in Vero Beach and show them one day when I go visit them." The light blue cover featured a Black girl looking a lot like Layla.

"Is this you?" Alex asked.

"¡Sí!" Layla said, happy that she had been recognized. "One of my cousins drew it. Oye, is that a tattoo?" she asked Ella, pushing her big round glasses up to her eyes to get a closer look.

"Oh, yes!" Ella said, lifting her sleeve up even more to show off her turtle tattoo.

"*Que bonito*," Layla said, admiring it up close.

Alex took one look at his sister's new tattoo and said, "Fun fact: a turtle, or *honu*, in Polynesian culture, is a symbol of health, peace, and longevity in life, among many other positive meanings."

"Cool!" Ella said, now even prouder of her addition.

"I love it!" Layla said, looking at Ella.

"Thank you, it took a while to convince my mamma to let me keep getting tattoos," Ella said, admiring her artful arm.

"How did you convince her?" Layla asked.

"I told her the truth: I want to express my inner world," Ella explained.

"Her inner world is quite different from mine," Alex said, smiling at Ella. "Even though we're twins."

"Wait, you're twins?" Layla said, her tone a bit louder than she intended.

The twins nodded yes.

"But you don't look alike!" Layla said.

"We know," Ella and Alex said in unison. If only they had a quarter for every single time people told them they didn't look alike, they would be able to play at the gumball machines for hours upon end! Why were people so shocked to learn they were twins, anyway? Did they really believe that being twins only meant looking alike on the outside?

"We are actually more alike than we seem to be," Ella said. "I'm just a bit smarter than him, that's all," she said with a grin.

Alex rolled his eyes and said, "Alright, enough with the chitchat. Let's go try our luck at the gumball machines. Race you there!" Then, he sprinted away.

The girls looked at one another.

"Ready?" Ella asked.

"Set, go!" Layla shouted, as they darted for the lobby.

the Dinosaur Tattoo

"A DINOSAUR!" LAYLA SCREAMED at the top of her lungs with delight as soon as she saw the tattoo that she won from the gumball machine. "I love dinosaurs!"

"Me too!" Alex said. "Fun fact: the word dinosaur is made up of two Greek words and it means Terrible Lizard. An English paleontologist came up with the name. I want to be a paleontologist when I grow up. No wait, an astronaut. Or a space engineer. Or a scientist. I'm not sure yet."

"I would love to be a writer," Layla said, swaying to the ukulele sound of *plink plink chiky plink*. "Ella, what do you want to be when you grow up?"

"A person who saves endangered animal species across the globe, or maybe an oceanographer, or a geologist, or a rockstar!" Ella said, playing on her invisible guitar. "That's why I want to ask Mamma if I can start taking guitar lessons. I'm going to travel all over the world and people are going to love my music, because I'm going to sing about saving animals and reducing pollution."

"That's so cool!" Layla said. "I want to learn how to play the drums."

"Seriously?" Alex said.

Layla nodded.

"You two could form a band and I could be your biggest fan and we could all travel together and be the Discovery Kids," Alex shouted, arms up in the air. "Get it? Because we met at Discovery Casa?"

"That's a great idea!" Ella said.

"And I could write about us in my Discovery Diary, and we could all have dinosaur tattoos," Layla suggested. "The dinosaur could be our logo."

"Yeah," Alex said. "Awesome idea!"

"Speaking of tattoos," Ella said. "Let's go to the bathroom so we can get that tattoo on you."

"Yay!" Layla said. "Wait, is it going to hurt?"

"Not even a tiny bit," Ella reassured her. "We just need some water."

"*Phew!*" Layla said. "When we're done, we should go and show my grandmother!"

"Sounds good," Alex said. "What's her name?"

"You can just call her Abuelita," Layla said.

CHAPTER 4

Abuelita

"ALEX, ELLA, THIS IS *mi abuelita,*" Layla said.

Abuelita was sitting by the café in the plaza where she was enjoying a tall glass of *chicha,* an oat beverage typical of Panama.

"OK, WOW!" Ella exclaimed as soon as she saw her. "That is a *stunning* dress. It actually looks recycled, which is even cooler, as it gives purpose to what many people consider waste."

"*Muchas gracias, mi querida,*" Abuelita said as she stood up, grabbed her skirt on each side, and flared it to show off her outfit even better. It was made of different, colorful fabrics sewn together in harmony. "This is the dress I made for the *Pollera Conga,* a Panamanian festival that celebrates our African heritage."

"You used all the colors but red," Alex noticed as he admired Abuelita's dress.

"*Muy bien, mi hijo,* you have a good eye. We don't use red in our *piezas*," Abuelita explained, pointing at the fabrics. "In our Congolese culture, red symbolizes the *chamuco*."

"Evil," Layla offered a translation.

"The flowers in your hair are so beautiful," Ella said.

"Thank you," Abuelita said, lightly touching the wildflowers she had above her ears and behind her head. "The flowers are called *Cañitolendo* and they come from the Costa Arriba and Costa Abajo in Panama."

"What are your necklaces made of?" Alex asked, looking at the many necklaces that Abuelita was wearing, which accentuated her vibrant and lively outfit even more.

"Some are made with beads, some with shells, and some with seeds," she explained.

"Is the *Pollera Conga* today then?" Ella asked.

Abuelita shook her head. "No, but life and culture must be celebrated every day, *mi hija*. Especially when you are far away from your home country. You have to keep your heritage alive, or you risk losing who you are."

"That's what Mamma says," Alex said. "Fun fact: Our grandparents came from southern Italy—Naples, to be specific—and we keep our heritage alive every day through the food Mamma cooks, which is *molto buono*, and the many family stories behind every dish she prepares!"

"Bravo," Abuelita said. "Food is culture."

The four of them sat at the table and Abuelita ordered *chicha* for her guests. "Layla, is that a tattoo?" she asked, looking at her granddaughter's arm.

"*Si*, Abuelita." Layla explained. "*¿Te gusta?*"

"*Claro que si, mi amor*, I like it a lot." Abuelita said, "It's art."

"Yes, finally!" Ella stated in exasperation, her arms stretched out in front of her. "Tattoos *are* art, *thank you!*"

"*De nada*," Abuelita smiled. "Speaking of art, have you heard of our new resident?"

The children shook their head.

"Not many people have," she said, leaning closer to the children and lowering her voice as if about to reveal a big secret. "All we know is that his name is Art. He doesn't speak to anybody and always keeps to himself. I even invited him to my dance class, but he didn't come."

The children, now enjoying their chicha, looked at one another, their eyebrows raised. *Who was this mysterious new resident?*

Looking for Art

Kuku-Kuku.

The plaza cuckoo clock struck four in the afternoon.

"Oh, it's time for my *cumbia* dance class," Abuelita said, standing up. "I must go, my students are waiting for me."

"You *teach* the dance class?" Alex asked.

"*Sí, mi hijo.*" Abuelita said, smiling and swaying from side to side. "Would you like to join us?"

"*Ehm* . . ." Alex forced a smile, trying to hide his fear of dancing in public. "Maybe next time."

"Well then," Abuelita said, flaring her skirt once more. "*Besitos a todos*, kisses everyone, it's *fiesta* time!" And off she went.

"Your grandmother is a lot of fun!" Ella said to Layla.

Layla smiled.

"So, what do we do now?" Alex asked, leaning back in his chair.

"I don't know," Ella said. "I don't have any more quarters."

"I don't either," Layla echoed, tapping her empty jeans pockets.

"So, no gumball machines," Alex said with a heavy sigh.

Silence blanketed the Discovery Kids for a few moments.

"Hey, what if we went on a mission to find out more about Art, the new resident?" Ella asked.

"Yes!" Alex said, sitting up quickly.

"But where should we begin?" Layla asked.

Alex shrugged.

"Let's walk around and see," Ella said.

The three friends stood up, placed their chairs under the table, and threw away their empty cups.

"I wish they'd stop using plastic," Ella commented after throwing her cup away. "It's so bad for the environment and the animal kingdom."

Alex and Layla nodded in agreement. Then, they began walking around the plaza in the hope of discovering more about the mysterious resident.

"Maybe he likes to play in the arcade?" Alex suggested.

"Let's go there and see," Layla said.

But when they arrived, they found a yellow sign on the floor at the entrance that read: Caution, Wet Floor.

"They just cleaned the arcade," Ella noticed. "So, we can't go in there and clearly he's not here," she said, referring to the empty room.

"Maybe he's playing bocce," Alex said.

"Oh, good idea," Layla said. "Let's go and see."

But no luck there either, as the bocce court was empty.

"Well, he's not at the café, or the arcade, or playing bocce," Alex said. "Where could he be?"

"Maybe he's in his casa," Layla said.

Alex, Ella, and Layla glanced at one another and headed for the residents' quarters. They were determined to find Art.

They walked for what felt like an eternity. And the more they walked, the more they couldn't find him. Resigned, they kept wandering the many closed doors of the residents' homes framing their tedious voyage.

"This is boring," Alex whispered.

Layla sighed heavily.

"We have to have patience, guys," Ella reminded them. "Like when I wait for baby turtles to hatch on the beach. It takes time, but the wait is worth it."

"Hey, look!" Alex said, planting his feet in front of a casa whose door was slightly open.

Ella and Layla stopped to look at what caught Alex's attention in that room: a painting.

the Painting

"ARE THOSE . . . dinosaurs?" Ella asked, looking at the painting.

"Plesiosaurus, to be precise," Layla stated to the surprise of the twins who turned to look at her with eyes wide open.

Attracted by the painting, she walked into the room to take a closer look. The details on the dinosaurs were incredible: the plesiosaurus had its signature long neck—so long, in fact, that it was half the length of its body—and small head.

"You can't just walk into someone's casa," Alex said.

"I just want to take a look at the painting," Layla justified herself.

"Me too," Ella said.

"Mamma is going to be upset when she finds out," Alex said, but Ella had already followed her new friend into the house.

Alex glanced at the mailbox and noticed there was no name on it. He looked left and right, but there was no one in sight. "Maybe this isn't someone's casa," he whispered.

"What a mess!" Ella said, catching Alex's attention. He stepped into the room as well, slightly closing the door behind him, and looked at what must have been hundreds of paintbrushes and oil painting tubes of the most varied colors scattered everywhere. "This is messier than your room, Alex."

Alex nodded in agreement.

"Is this a new art room?" Layla asked, looking at the large blue blanket that covered the carpeted floor. Judging by the countless colorful paint spatters—some sunshine yellow, some ocean blue, some forest green—the blanket must have been placed there to avoid staining the actual carpet. The same couldn't be said of the once white walls, which now looked more like polka-dotted rainbow walls.

"I don't think so," Ella said. "Look, this is clearly a casa." She pointed to the bed in the corner, which had been properly made—the only tidy thing in the entire casa.

"But whose casa is this?" Alex asked. "If someone actually lived here, wouldn't they have family photos on the walls like all the other residents? Instead, there are only dinosaur drawings everywhere."

Layla shrugged.

"Fun fact, there were over 700 species of dinosaurs!" Alex said.

"But why are the dinosaurs at the beach, that couldn't have been the best for the environment," Ella wondered out loud, looking back at the painting. "And why is there a woman with them?"

"¿Qué?" Layla gasped, getting closer to the painting as well, with Alex right behind her. "¡Una mujer!"

"A woman?" Alex echoed.

Indeed, kneeling among the dinosaurs—and therefore, barely visible—on the beach was a woman holding a hammer and chisel, a basket placed next to her. She wore a long dress with a matching shawl and a bonnet.

"Wait, we all learned in school that human beings didn't exist when dinosaurs roamed the earth," Alex said.

"I think the woman in there is a mistake," Ella said.

"I don't care if it's a mistake," Layla said, her mouth open in admiration. "I love it! I am going to draw it in my Discovery Diary."

"No, I think we should leave," Alex said. "We are not supposed to be here, and we'll get in trouble if Mamma finds us."

But in that very moment, the door squeaked open.

The children quickly turned toward it, gasping in shock when they saw an old man in a white coat standing at the threshold.

That's when his name appeared on the door: *Art.*

the Painting

"UHM, GOO-GOOD AFTERNOO-OON SIR," Alex said. "We were just about to leave."

A black and white mustache and wavy wrinkles decorated Art's face, which was framed by gray hair and an artist beret. His white coat was stained with paint and seemed to perfectly match the polka-dotted walls; with his pockets full of paintbrushes, he slowly walked inside the casa and his long and pointy shoes made an odd *skreek skreek* sound with every step he took.

"Sir, did you paint this?" Ella asked, pointing at the dinosaur painting.

He nodded and a hint of a smile creased his face.

"It's beautiful!" Layla said.

"But why is there a woman there?" Ella said, hands on hips. "I don't think that's correct, sir. See, human beings were not around when the dinosaurs were here."

Art sighed. Then, he picked a paint palette from the floor and gave a paintbrush to Ella, who accepted it.

Ella looked at the paintbrush as if she had never seen a paintbrush before. Well, she had seen paintbrushes before, but *this* one was different: the bristle was made of soft brown hair and the blue handle was unusually bendy, as if made of rubber rather than wood or plastic.

"Ella, let's just go," Alex said in a trembling voice, pulling her arm and turning toward the door. "Sir, thank you for your time and we apologize for walking in your roo—"

But a sudden gust of wind closed the door shut, making the children gasp.

They turned to look at the old man, who tapped on the palette. The oil paint quickly gathered to form letters the children didn't understand:

$$\text{תמא}$$

Staring at him with their mouths dry, they heard a whisper: *Emet*. But nobody in the room had spoken . . . so where did that voice come from?

Emet

Emet

Emet

Emet

Emet

The mysterious voice echoed.

What did it mean?

Alex, Ella, and Layla held hands and scootched close to one another. Art closed his eyes, smiled, and blew over the paint, creating an explosion of color that filled the room. The paintbrush that Ella was still holding shimmered and projected its light through the bristles onto the dinosaur woman, who was now glowing. The paint twirled faster and faster, creating a vortex that yanked Alex, Ella, and Layla off the ground, making them spin uncontrollably.

The last thing they saw was a bright beam of colorful light.

The last thing they heard was *Emet*.

CHAPTER 8

Emet

FA-THUD!

Alex, Ella, and Layla fell to the ground.

"Ouch!" Ella said, massaging her back as she sat up, still holding on the paintbrush.

Dizzy and sore and more than a little frightened, the children looked at one another.

"Where are we?" Alex asked, studying his surroundings: imposing cliffs overlooked the thin strip of land the children had landed on. In front of them was the sea. It was windy and the choppy waters created raging white caps on the surface. The wind blew from the sea, splashing the salty taste of the ocean on the children's faces. The sky, covered by dark gray clouds, decided not to let any sunlight through and made it harder for the Discovery Kids to find out where they were.

"The beach?" Layla suggested, patting the sand off her clothes.

"This doesn't look like the beaches in Vero Beach though . . ." Ella said.

"It isn't, dah'ling," the paintbrush said.

"*AAAH!*" Ella screamed at the top of her lungs, throwing the talking paintbrush in the sand.

"What's wrong?" Alex and Layla said in unison, running closer to Ella, who was shaking like a leaf and pointing to the sand.

"Th-th-the p-p-paintbrush talked!" she managed to say.

"Oh-kay," Alex said, rolling his eyes. "How hard did you hit your head?"

"It *did* talk!" Ella insisted. She knew she sounded totally coo coo, but it was the truth!

Layla walked toward the paintbrush. She was about to pick it up when—

"Pardon me, dah'ling, but would you mind *not* throwing me in the sand next time?" the paintbrush said, whipping his hair back and forth. "It gets caught in my fabulous hair and I don't quite care for it."

"*AAAH!*" the children screamed in unison.

"Oh dear," the paintbrush said, shaking sand out of his hair. "I told Art you'd react this way."

"Who are you and where are we and why can you talk and what are we doing here?" Alex asked all in one breath.

"Oh dear, where are my manners," the paintbrush said. "My name is Emet, *enchanté.*" He bowed. "We are in Lyme Regis, south of England, and the year is 1830."

The children were lost for words—yes, even Alex. They stared at Emet, who added: "I gather you have never time-travelled before?"

The children shook their head.

"Well," Emet said, "It can be rather daunting, especially the first time. But no need to worry, dah'lings. You'll soon get used to it."

"But why are we here?" Ella asked. "And would you please be careful with your colorful hair? I don't want to risk polluting such a pristine environment."

Emet whipped his hair back, to alleviate Ella's concerns. He was about to explain the reason for their voyage when—

"*Tray!*" a voice called from afar.

The children turned in the direction of the voice and saw a dog running toward a woman. Emet hid inside the pocket of Ella's sleeveless jacket—dogs gave him the heebie-jeebies.

Alex, Ella, and Layla looked at the woman, who wore a long dress with a matching shawl and a bonnet.

Just like the woman in the painting.

the Woman in the Painting

"WHO IS SHE?" LAYLA asked.

"No idea," Ella said. "But she looks just like the woman in the painting."

"Good thing the dinosaurs aren't here," Alex said in a trembling voice, quickly looking around to make sure he was right.

"*Rooff, rooff,*" the dog barked in the distance, pawing at the sand as if trying to dig up something.

"Let's go find out who she is," Ella said.

"No!" Alex said. "Mamma says not to talk to strangers."

"If I may, dah'lings," Emet said, emerging from the pocket "One should live at least for curiosity."

The children scratched their heads.

"What do you mean?" Alex asked.

"I mean, you should go and ask her," Emet explained.

Ella and Layla smiled and began walking toward the woman, with Alex slowly following behind them, muttering under his breath that this was a bad, bad idea. The wind was blowing stronger and stronger, and aside from them and the mysterious woman and her dog, there was nobody else on the beach. Once the children were close enough to the woman, who was kneeling on the sand, they noticed she was handling the same tools that Art had painted, a hammer and chisel, and had a basket by her side.

"Oh, good morning," the woman said as soon as she saw them. "Are you here for treasures?"

Alex, Ella, and Layla quickly glanced at one another, at a loss for words.

CHAPTER 10

Treasures

"TREASURES?" ALEX ASKED. HE looked around, expecting to see treasure chests filled with gold doubloons. But no such luck.

"Yes," the woman said, cleaning mud off a small rock. "Look, this is a snakestone." She showed them what looked like a spiral shell petrified in the rock. It was elegant and well defined.

"That's a fossil!" Layla shouted, her eyes gleaming with joy at the sight of a real fossil. She was about to draw its shape in her Discovery Diary when she realized she didn't have it with her. "Maybe it couldn't time travel," she whispered to herself.

Emet peeked out of Ella's pocket and seeing that the dog wasn't that close to them, jumped out of it to see what the children were looking at. "To be precise, dah'lings, that is an ammonite," Emet whispered before jumping in Ella's pocket again, just to be safe. "A prehistoric sea creature."

"Fun fact, there are many types of fossils, not just ammonites," Alex said as he was kneeling to get a closer look at the fossil Emet had just described.

"Where did you find it?" Layla asked.

"There are many treasures here," the woman said. "Would you like to buy this one?"

"Nah, we used all our quarters on the gumball machines," Ella explained.

"*Ahem*, 1830," Emet whispered, gently poking Ella in the chest.

"I mean, we have no money," Ella said, offering a broad smile.

"Much better, dah'ling," Emet whispered.

"How do you find fossils?" Layla asked, paying attention to every detail so she could write it all down in her Discovery Diary when she eventually got back home.

"Oh, it is a long process," the woman said. "It takes many hours of hard work, every single day. No matter the weather, which is why I am here today, even though it's so windy. As a matter of fact, it is best to hunt for fossils when it is rainy or windy because this weather cleans the rocks, and one might spot fossils a bit more easily."

"It sure is windy now," Ella said, her colorful hair waving in the wind. "Can you show us how to look for treasures, without doing harm to the environment?"

"Of course! Let's begin with looking at these small rocks," she said, pointing at the many pebbles and rocks that were mixed with the sand. "You want to look for uneven surfaces, any marks that seem out of place."

"Cool! I'm Alex, by the way," Alex made introductions, now feeling more at ease with the woman. "And this is my twin sister Ella and our friend Layla."

"Pleased to meet you, Alex, Ella, and Layla. This is Tray," she said, looking at her dog who was wagging his tail with excitement. "And my name is Mary Anning."

CHAPTER 11

Mary Anning

PEBBLE BY PEBBLE, THE children looked for treasures.

"Nope," Alex said, looking at a small rock. "Nope," he said again, placing another pebble back on the sand.

Alas, each pebble they picked was smooth and had no odd marks on it.

"This sure takes time," Ella said. "Not as much as cleaning the beaches and picking up all the trash people leave there, but still takes time."

"Indeed," Mary Anning said. "And loads of patience. But trust me, we are surrounded by treasures and finding one makes it all worth it in the end."

"Are you from here, Miss Anning?" Alex asked.

"Oh, please call me Mary," she said. "Yes, I am from Lyme Regis. Are you from Lyme Regis as well?"

"Nah, we're from the United States and time-trav—," Ella was interrupted by another gentle poke from Emet.

"United States of America?" Mary Anning said. "You must have had a long and rocky journey in these waters."

"You have no idea," Ella whispered, still feeling a bit sore from the fall.

"So, is this your job, Mary?" Layla asked, as she kept looking through the pebbles and rocks.

"Yes, indeed," Mary Anning said. "My father taught me when I was very little. We used to come here all the time and find treasures together. Then, we would sell them. I have lost count of how many treasures we sold, some big, some small."

Sniff sniff, Tray trotted closer to Layla and pawed at the sand as if trying to help his new fossil hunters. Then, he wagged his tail, stuck his tongue out, and looked at Mary.

In that same moment, Layla held up an oddly shaped rock and shouted, "I found a fossil!"

the Fossil

LAYLA HELD THE ROCK up high as if it were a golden trophy.

Ella and Alex gasped at the sight, and Emet peeked out of the pocket once again to see what she had found.

"Oh, let's have a look!" Mary Anning said, looking closer at Layla's treasure. Then, she wrinkled her nose and smiled.

"What is it?" Layla asked, feeling her heart beating faster with anticipation.

"This is a bezoar," Mary Anning said.

Layla cocked her head, Alex scratched his, and Ella frowned.

Emet fell back in the pocket and let out a hearty belly laugh.

"What's that?" Layla asked.

"*Ehm . . .*" Mary Anning hesitated before saying, "It's fossilized poop."

"*Ewww!*" Layla said, quickly letting go of it.

"Why, it is a good discovery," Mary Anning said. "I wish I had a brush with me to polish it off for you."

"Oh," Ella said. "I have a bru—"

Another poke from Emet stopped Ella right in her tracks.

"Ouch!" Ella said between her teeth and looking down at her pocket. "You have got to stop doing that."

"Pardon, dah'ling," Emet whispered.

"Fun fact," Alex said. "Fossilized poop can tell us a whole lot about the creature it came from, including what they ate!"

"That is true, Alex," Mary Anning said. "That's what I told the many scientists when I showed them my discovery, and they didn't believe me."

"Why not?" he asked.

"Well, they laughed at me and told me that as a lady, I should not be talking about poop and that I did not know what I was talking about because this clearly was not what I thought it was. So, you know what I did?"

The children stared at her, their mouths open with curiosity.

"I told them that yes, I am a lady, but I am also a scientist. And as such, I do know what I am talking about and even showed them all my notes and studies. It took them some time, but eventually they realized I was right."

"Yeah, you showed them!" Ella said, hands on hips.

"It's so sad that they didn't believe you," Layla said, shaking her head.

"Oh, I wasn't surprised. It happened many times before," Mary Anning said.

"When?" Alex asked.

"It's a long story, one that requires me to have my notes, which are in my fossil depot. Would you like to join me there?"

"Yes!" the children said in unison.

"Jolly good," she said, placing the ammonite and bezoar in her basket and gathering her chisel and hammer. "Shall we?"

The children followed behind her as Tray ran ahead to make way.

CHAPTER 13

the Fossil Depot

"THIS IS FOSSIL HEAVEN!" Layla said, looking around Mary Anning's fossil depot, which was nothing more than a small room with a wooden desk, two chairs, and white walls covered with shelves filled with fossils. Each fossil properly polished and proudly displayed, marked with a short description of what it represented.

"I love all these seashells," Alex said, looking at the countless small seashells that decorated the room.

Emet took a peek at the fossil depot, making sure to stay as hidden as possible in Ella's pocket. But even he couldn't help but marvel at what he saw.

"Thank you," Mary Anning said to Alex. "I often sell them by the seashore."

"Like the nursery rhyme!" Ella whispered, "She sells seashells by the seashore."

Alex and Layla smiled at her, while Mary Anning opened a drawer and took out several papers, spreading them out on the desk. "Shall we begin?"

"Yes!" The children said in unison.

"This is a fish lizard," Mary Anning said, pointing to a paper that had a drawing of a skeleton and a few notes on it. "I found it when I was eleven years old."

"Whoa!" Alex said, looking at the drawing. "This is huge!"

"Oh, it was!" Mary Anning said, "My brother helped me dig it out of the mud and dirt, and it was so heavy that the villagers had to help us carry it home. But they were scared because it was big with hundreds of teeth and long jaws."

"They were scared of the fossil?" Layla asked her, looking closely at the details so she could sketch it in her Discovery Diary later on.

"Yes, they said I had discovered a monster, but I knew they were wrong."

"How did you know what it was?" Ella asked. "Did you learn it in school?"

"Well, I didn't go to school," Mary Anning said.

"What!?" Alex asked, his eyebrows raised in surprise. "Why not?"

"My family was very poor, and school was too expensive," Mary Anning said, looking down at her papers and adjusting herself in the chair. "But I read many books and learned on my own." She looked up at the children with a big smile across her face.

"Where is the fish lizard now?" Ella asked.

"Well, a gentleman bought it and donated it to a museum in London," Mary Anning explained.

"What's this one?" Alex asked, pointing at another drawing.

"The flying dragon," Mary Anning said. "I found it two years ago and was shocked when I saw it had wings!"

"A flying dragon?" Layla asked, furrowing her eyebrows.

Mary Anning nodded yes. "Look, I also found a reptile," she said, showing them one more drawing.

Knock knock.

Somebody was at the door.

"*Rooff rooff,*" Tray barked.

"Oh, I wonder who that might be," Mary Anning said, standing up.

The children wondered too.

She walked to the door, opened it, and was met by a man wearing a black suit and a black top hat, which he took off as soon as he saw the woman.

"He came in a carriage?" Ella wondered out loud, looking at the large, horse-drawn black wagon behind the gentleman. "No smog, that's awesome!"

"Pardon me, I shall be right back," Mary Anning said, glancing back at her guests. Then, she stepped outside her fossil depot, followed by Tray, and closed the door behind her.

"I cannot believe it," Layla said, staring at Mary Anning's drawings.

"What?" Ella asked.

"The reptile is a plesiosaurus, like the dinosaurs in the painting."

"Oh wow . . ." Alex whispered. "You're right."

"What?" Ella asked. "Does this mean that *she* was the one who discovered them?"

"If I may, dah'lings," Emet said, clearing his voice and jumping out of Ella's pocket and on to the desk. "I believe the time has come for me to reveal the truth with a stroke of magic."

a Stroke of Magic

EMET TOOK A DEEP breath, closed his eyes, and began shimmering. The children, scootching closer together and holding hands, gasped as his glow intensified and projected a rainbow of colors all over the room. As if immersed in a motion picture, the children looked all around them and saw a little girl.

"Mary Anning was born May 21, 1799," Emet began narrating, as images of her childhood scrolled by. "When she was a little over a year old, she was struck by lightning but, fortunately, survived."

Images of Mary Anning and her father digging for fossils appeared throughout the room. "Even after her father fell ill and passed away, Mary Anning kept digging for fossils and discovered something incredible: an ichthyosaur! Soon, other amazing findings followed: plesiosaur and pterodactyl!"

Projected throughout the room were Mary Anning's drawings. To the children's surprise, the drawings began taking their real-life shapes and soon turned into actual dinosaurs! Alex, Ella, and Layla gasped as they admired the mighty animals that Mary Anning had discovered. Layla even reached out with her hand toward the walls, as if trying to touch the dinosaurs.

"Lyme Regis, where Mary has lived her whole life, is home to over 185 million years of dinosaur history."

"Whoa!" Alex whispered as images of many different dinosaur species appeared across the walls.

"Lyme Regis is a truly special place for geologists and paleontologists," Emet said. "Nowhere else in the whole world have fossils from the Triassic, Jurassic, and Cretaceous eras been found in the same place."

Then, Emet shimmered brighter and projected the image of Mary Anning at the beach, kneeling among the plesiosaurus, holding a hammer and chisel, with a wicker basket by her side.

"Art's painting!" Ella, Layla, and Alex shouted in unison. They looked all around the room at the large images that surrounded them and felt as though they had truly jumped into the painting.

"Indeed dah'lings," Emet said, smiling and twirling. "It is thanks to Mary Anning's discoveries that scientists have learned so much more about Earth, evolution, and prehistoric life. But history has forgotten her name . . ."

Emet's tone turned somber, and darkness engulfed the room.

The children gasped.

"Because she was a woman from a poor family, men bought fossils she found and took credit for her discoveries, inserting *their* names into the history books," Emet said. "But she never gave up." A dim candlelight illuminated the room and a grown Mary Anning appeared at her desk studying. "She kept studying and discovering fossils."

With that, images of Mary Anning disappeared, and Emet drew three floating letters across the room:

תמא

The children looked in awe.

"These three letters mean Truth," Emet said. "And you now know what the truth is."

Alex, Ella, and Layla nodded with a smile.

"But I must warn you, dah'lings," Emet whispered, "the truth is a heavy burden to carry, a burden that only children can endure. And you must do right by it by telling the truth about who Mary Anning was and the role she played in the history of humanity."

The children exchanged a determined look.

But in that moment, the doorknob turned.

"I shall bid farewell to the Geological Society of London if they fail to recognize me for my achievements!" Mary Anning shouted before storming into the room.

CHAPTER 15

Recognizing Mary Anning

POOF!

The letters disappeared, the room looked like nothing ever happened, and Emet jumped back inside Ella's pocket.

"Oh-hi-hi-hey," Alex mumbled.

Mary Anning slammed the door behind her and said, "That man came to tell me that my request to join the Geological Society of London has been rejected—again. All because I am a woman."

The children listened quietly.

"Yet all their members come here and ask me to take them to the cliffs and teach them how to look for fossils." Mary Anning plopped down on the chair, Tray placing his head on her lap.

The children exchanged a knowing look. They knew exactly what to do.

"History won't forget about you," Layla said with a smile.

"We will make sure of it." Alex echoed.

"But you can't give up now," Ella said.

Mary Anning sighed. "How can you be so sure?"

"Because we now know the truth and we know who you are," Layla said, as Ella and Alex nodded in agreement.

"Very well then," Mary Anning said, standing up. "I shall go and speak with that gentleman once more and tell him that I will keep requesting to join the Geological Society of London, come what may."

The children cheered her on, and she walked outside the depot, Tray trotting after her.

"If history won't give her the recognition she deserves and insert *her* name in the books, I will," Layla stated. "I will write about her in my Discovery Diary, as soon as we get back home."

It was in that moment that Emet shimmered and created an explosion of colors that twirled faster and faster, generating a vortex that yanked Alex, Ella, and Layla off the ground.

It was time to go back.

CHAPTER 16

Back at Discovery Casa

FA-THUD!

"Ouch!" Ella said, massaging her back that hurt from the fall. Again.

"Discovery Casa!" Alex shouted, recognizing the colorful casa with Mary Anning's painting.

"My Discovery Diary!" Layla said, quickly grabbing the notebook that had been sitting on the floor.

Skreek skreek.

Alex, Ella, and Layla immediately recognized the sound and turned to look at him.

"Mr. Art!" Alex said, feeling strangely at a loss for words. He didn't know if he should thank Art for such a wonderful adventure, if he should apologize for still being in his casa, or if he should ask him questions about Emet and his stroke of magic.

Art must have sensed his hesitation and gave him a reassuring smile.

"That was *Ah*-Mazing!" Ella said, throwing her hands up in the air as if she just got off a thrilling rollercoaster ride. "And very smog-free, too, since we didn't use any fuel to travel."

"I can't wait to write about it in my Discovery Diary," Layla said, her eyes sparkling with joy.

"Dah'lings!" Emet said, popping out of the pocket in Art's white coat. He jumped on Art's right shoulder and tickled Art's mustache with his brown hair, making him giggle.

"Emet!" The children greeted him in unison.

"What an absolutely fabulous adventure that was!" Emet said.

The children nodded in agreement.

"Now remember," Emet said. "You must do right by the truth."

"We will," the children promised.

"But wait," Layla suddenly remembered. "Did the Geological Society of London ever recognize Mary Anning for her many discoveries?"

"They did, dah'ling," Emet said, his tone revealing sadness. "But only after her death."

"Oh no . . ." the children said in unison.

Art and Emet looked down, as silence fell upon them.

"Don't worry," Abuelita said, walking into Art's casa. "What matters is that now you know her story and the role she played in history."

"Abuelita!" Layla said, hugging her.

"*Hola, mi hija,*" Abuelita said, smiling at her granddaughter. "Did you have fun?"

"Wait, how long have you been standing there for?" Alex asked.

"Let's just say, I loved witnessing your adventure." Abuelita winked. "*No te preocupes,* I can keep a secret."

Art smiled at her, and the Discovery Kids released a sigh of relief.

But the relief was soon replaced by fear when they heard a familiar voice.

"*Aleeex, Ellaaaa.*"

"That's Mamma!" Alex and Ella said in unison.

"*Where are you?*" Mamma sounded both scared and upset that she couldn't find the twins. "*It's time to go home!*"

CHAPTER 17

Time to Go Home

"MAMMA!" ALEX AND ELLA stepped outside Art's casa and greeted her.

"Oh, there you are!" Mamma shouted as soon as she saw Alex and Ella. "I've been looking everywhere for you. What are you doing here?" Mamma said, glancing at the inside of Art's casa. "How many times have I told you not—"

"Oh, it's my fault," Abuelita interrupted her. "I brought them here to show them Art's beautiful painting of Mary Anning and her dinosaurs."

"Who?" Mamma asked.

"Alex and Ella will tell you all about her," Abuelita said, winking at them.

"Or you can read it in my Discovery Diary once I'm done writing about it," Layla said.

"I'd love to," Mamma said, smiling at Layla.

"Sorry Mamma," the twins said. "We didn't mean to worry you."

"It's OK," Mamma said, smiling at them. Then, she looked at Art and tilted her head. "Are you the new resident?"

Art nodded, placing a hand over his coat pocket where Emet was hiding.

"You look so familiar . . ." Mamma said, furrowing her eyebrows and trying to remember. "I feel like we have met before."

Alex and Ella looked at their mamma, then back at Art, and their furrowed foreheads revealed curiosity.

"Have we?" Mamma asked.

Art glanced around as if looking for an answer.

"Oh well, I guess it'll come to me," Mamma said. "Alright you two, it's time to go home now."

The children, Mamma, and Abuelita waved goodbye to Art, who waved back. Then, while Mamma and Abuelita walked ahead together, Alex, Ella, and Layla turned to look back at Art's casa once more. That's when they saw Emet's brown hair pop up from inside Art's pocket.

"Goodbye, Emet," the children said in a low tone.

"Until next time, my dah'lings," Emet whispered.

a New Stroke of Magic

"COME ON, MAMMA, HURRY!" Ella said, her leg jittering with anticipation.

"Why are you two in such a rush to get to Discovery Casa?" Mamma asked, as she parked the car and turned the engine off.

"We'll explain later, love you!" the twins zoomed out of the car and ran to the entrance.

Plink plink chiky plink.

The ukulele music welcomed them.

"Where did Layla say to meet her?" Alex asked Ella as he ran ahead of his sister.

"At the plaza," Ella replied, trying to keep up with her brother.

Kuku-Kuku

The cuckoo clock stroke four in the afternoon.

A few moments later, they saw Layla sitting alone at the café, drumming her fingers on the table. Alex and Ella quickly sat down next to her.

After hellos had been exchanged, Ella said, "We got the note you left us in my locker at school."

"It said to come meet you here today at this time," Alex said. "What's going on?"

"Abuelita called me," Layla whispered, leaning forward. "She said Art finished a new painting."

Alex and Ella gasped.

"A new stroke of magic?" Alex wondered out loud.

"Only one way to find out," Ella said with a grin.

Alex, Ella, and Layla got up and made their way to Art's casa.

A new adventure was on the horizon.

• A C K N O W L E D G E M E N T S •

THE PROCESS OF WRITING this book has been both fun and challenging. Fortunately for me, I have had great companions by my side who have inspired, supported, and encouraged me along the way.

To my talented illustrator, Valerio Mazzoli. When you first showed me your drawing of a Nonno with three children on a fun adventure among dinosaurs and asked me to write a story about it, I never imagined it would turn out to be this one. I am extremely proud of the book we have created and the magical story we brought to life. Being able to say that you are my illustrator is a dream come true to me. *Grazie di cuore!*

To my amazing publisher, JuLee Brand. Thank you for taking the time to meet these characters and go with them on their fun and enchanting journey. Your unwavering support and love for this mischievous and curious bunch is what made this book possible.

To Blanca Icela Watts and the Panama Folklore Nonprofit Organization in Seattle, WA, for your help with creating the characters of Abuelita and Layla and allowing me to properly portray Afro-Panamanian culture. *¡Muchísimas gracias!*

To Vivian Kirkfield. Thank you for reading this story before it was a book and offering beautiful words of encouragement and precious suggestions on how to improve it even more. Your advice was invaluable.

To my Mamma, Babbo, and my sister Tiziana for always cheering me on and never forcing me to fit into a mold. The freedom you entrusted me with allowed me to embrace my creativity and harness my craft.

To my children, Alexander and Rossella. Your adventurous spirit, imagination, and endless creativity never cease to inspire and amaze me. Thank you for being the reason why I wrote this book.

To my beloved husband Michael, who's my support system, my best friend, and my casa. I know that the only reason why you are able to live with this writer is because of your unconditional love for me. Hold on to it . . . I'll be writing many more books.

To all my friends and family sprinkled across the world. Your loyalty, support, and affection mean everything to me.

To my readers, thank you for choosing to embark upon this adventure with Alex, Ella, and Layla. I hope you'll have fun!

Brunella Costagliola

Brunella Costagliola is an award-winning author, best-selling editor, and translator.

Raised in Bacoli, a small coastal town west of Naples, Southern Italy, Brunella is passionate about sharing her home country's culture, traditions, and history through her stories. Founder and owner of The Military Editor® Agency, LLC, a ghostwriting and editing agency catering to military authors and military-related manuscripts, Brunella helps fellow writers tell their stories and achieve their publishing dreams.

A proud mamma of her two Italian American children, who are an endless source of inspiration for her stories, and devoted Air Force wife to her now-retired husband, Brunella lives in Florida with her family and their three dogs.

Add your stroke of magic

to the following pages of illustrations

and if you email them to us,

we'll share them on our Instagram platform.

Be sure to tell us your name

and if you'd like to be tagged in the post.

Have fun!

www.themilitaryeditor.com

email: brunella@theitalianwriter.com